Having a Wonderful Time

ANANAS
POSTE
7s

3ᵈ POSTE
rose
ANANAS

ANANAS
cacao
2.s POSTE

18 VI
HAMM
1997

HAMM
1997
ANANA

TOM POHRT

FARRAR STRAUS GIROUX

NEW YORK

FOR SAM

Copyright © 1999 by Tom Pohrt
All rights reserved
Distributed in Canada by Douglas & McIntyre Ltd.
Color separations by Hong Kong Scanner Arts
Printed and bound in the United States of America by Berryville Graphics
Designed by Filomena Tuosto and Tom Pohrt
First edition, 1999

Library of Congress Cataloging-in-Publication Data
Pohrt, Tom.
    Having a wonderful time / Tom Pohrt. — 1st ed.
        p.   cm.
    Summary: While on vacation, Eva and her cat Sam end up at the
Crocodile Café where they find themselves on the following day's menu.
    ISBN 0-374-32898-6
    [1. Vacations—Fiction.   2. Cats—Fiction.]   I. Title.
PZ7.P75182Hav   1999
[E]—dc21   98-13093

It is another cold, dark winter day. Sam and
I are looking at a photograph in a magazine
which shows a beach with palm trees under
a sunny sky.

"Sam, why don't we take a vacation
someplace faraway and warm?"

"My thoughts exactly, Eva," Sam responds,
and he immediately begins to pack his
knapsack.

After getting the necessary travel shots
and checking to see that our passports are
in order, we book passage on the zeppelin
La Grande Banane.

From high up in the zeppelin, Sam and I
watch an ocean liner go by and a school of
whales send spouts into the air.

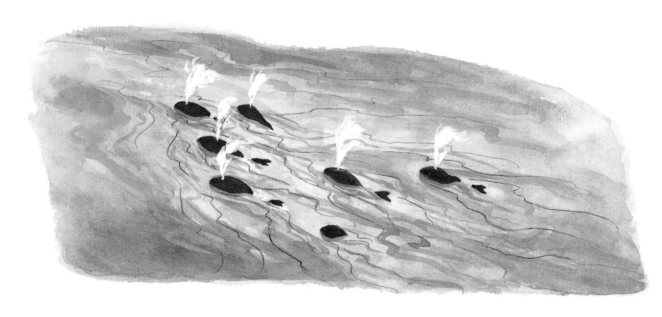

We write letters to friends while drinking mint tea and eating little wedge-shaped tuna-fish sandwiches for lunch. Sam loves to spend the afternoons sketching our fellow passengers.

After many days, *La Grande Banane* is
hovering over a beautiful city on a bay,
beside the sea. In the distance lies a
wide-open desert.

We've reached our destination.
Our airship lands and we
disembark as evening sets in.
Palm trees line the streets.

In an alley we find a small hotel.
"You are being given the *last* room
available in the entire city!" the proprietor
tells us.

Settling into bed, I discover a group of
insects camped under the sheets. Sam
startles some more tucked among towels
in a chest of drawers where he has made
his bed.

The proprietor, a lizard, joins the bugs
on the bed in a loud and raucous game
of dominoes.

I complain to the proprietor, who
responds, "Why, of course, booked
in advance, wonderful group!"

We end up sleeping on a bench in
a park overlooking the bay.

"*Coo-roo-coo, coo-roo-coo,*" say the pigeons who wake us early the following morning. Having had little rest and no bath, we find a small café and eat breakfast.

After our meal, we walk through the
outskirts of the city to look at the
monuments in the desert.

"One of the magnificent wonders of
the ancient world!" I exclaim to Sam.

"Better than a postcard" is Sam's reply.

A camel comes up to us. He
introduces himself as Cassis.
"I will be your guide and you
can ride upon my back," he says.

It is a cloudless day, and *we* are entranced
by the quality of the sunlight and the
vastness of the surrounding desert.

Camels have a very good sense of direction, except for Cassis, who soon tells us we are lost.

Farther on, we spy palm trees along the horizon.

"Maybe it's an oasis!" Sam shouts.

It is an oasis, and we drink from
a small pool of water.

When we look up, we are surprised to
see two lions fussing with a camera.

"Your picture taken?" the lions ask.

"Allow me to make a quick sketch of you
first," Sam replies.

Every vacation should be recorded with
at least one photograph. We hold very still
for the camera, trying to look as dignified
as possible.

Fragrant rosebushes surround us, so the
setting is extraordinary. But with flowers
come bees! And one buzzes about Sam's
head. He swats and misses, toppling into
a rosebush.

The bees are stirred up and we all run.
Fortunately, no one is stung. The bees
must have been as frightened as we were.
The lions are nowhere to be seen.

Riding from the oasis, we pass a signpost.
It reads: The Crocodile Café—due west as the
sun travels.

Having forgotten to pack a lunch, we are by now quite hungry.

The only sounds are Cassis's footpads against the stones and the growling of our stomachs.

No one is speaking.

Soon the gravel plain slopes gently
into a sandy valley.

A warm breeze carries the scent of jasmine
and lavender. We pass through a lush garden.
The *clink clank* of dishes mixed with loud
conversation greets our ears.

THE CROCODILE CAFÉ!
LUNCH AT LAST!

A regal-looking crocodile wearing a fez motions us to the café door.

"Welcome to the Crocodile Café. Table for two, right this way, if you please," he says, bowing deeply.

"What's the special of the day?" Sam asks as we are being seated.

"Why, *everything! Excellent choice!*" the crocodile waiter shouts, slapping his large, mossy palms together. *Clap! Clap!*

In an instant, a dozen crocodiles appear from the kitchen bearing large trays of delicious-smelling foods.

Sam and I just manage to get several bites of food down before the crocodile waiters whip the dishes out from under our chins.

"Dessert! Dessert!" shouts the crocodile with the fez.

But it soon becomes clear what the crocodiles are up to when we spy the following day's menu.